GABRIEL EVANS

A Human
for Kingsley

Little Hare
Hardie Grant Children's Publishing

For my sister, E, and your wonderful way with dogs.

Little Hare Books
an imprint of
Hardie Grant Children's Publishing
Wurundjeri Country
Ground Floor, Building 1, 658 Church Street
Richmond, Victoria 3121, Australia
www.hardiegrantchildrens.com

Text and illustrations copyright © Gabriel Evans 2021

First published 2021

A catalogue record for this
book is available from the
National Library of Australia

Hardie Grant acknowledges the Traditional Owners of the Country on which we work, the Wurundjeri
People of the Kulin Nation and the Gadigal People of the Eora Nation, and recognises their continuing
connection to the land, waters and culture. We pay our respects to their Elders past and present.

9781760506919 (hbk)

Designed by Pooja Desai

Printed in China through Asia Pacific Offset

10 9 8 7 6 5 4

Kingsley had decided to own a human.

It was not a decision to be taken lightly.
Owning a human was a BIG responsibility.

The problem was, there were so many humans to choose from – big or small, fast or slow, quiet or loud, happy or grumpy.

After meandering on the street for a while,

Kingsley picked a rather large, hairy one.

But filing reports was
tedious and slow.

I needed these
by yesterday!

Kingsley wasn't even sure what a report was.

Where are you going?
It's not even lunch!

So, he moved on.

Kingsley saw a human moving very fast.

He liked moving fast.

But this was ridiculous. So, he moved on.

He saw a human collecting hair and generously gave her some of his.

STOP THAT, YOU MUTT!

But she wasn't very grateful, and Kingsley had his pride.

So, he moved on.

Kingsley kept searching.

This human had too many small human subordinates.

This human just stood in one spot.

This human was too loud.

He didn't even stop
to consider *this* human.

There were so many humans to choose from.
But none of them were quite right, except …

… maybe this one.

Kingsley followed her.

She was a loud human.

Kingsley was intrigued.

Kingsley followed the
human to her home.

You can come in for a cup of water.

She had a very comfortable chair.

That's MY chair.

Or, as he now called it, *his* chair.

Boom!

Kingsley observed the little human carefully.

T-H-E B-I-G C-A-T S-A-T.

She seemed to have a lot of odd hobbies.

Push me.

Seesaw properly, buddy.

She was very demanding.

She had perplexing habits, like taking a bath – on purpose!

Kingsley liked this human.

But the question remained:

was she the right human for Kingsley?

He wasn't sure.

It's rude to stare, mister.

It was a conundrum.

Kingsley needed some time to think.

Kingsley didn't know what he wanted in a human.

Was he better off on his own?

There you are!

Did you get lost? I was so worried.

Come on, home is this way.

Maybe what Kingsley needed in a human was someone ...

... who needed him.

And that made all the difference.